The Six Stars Club

Written by: Dr Swaroop Rawal

Illustrated by: Suman S. Roy

Published by

Kuldeep Jain

for

Pegasus

An imprint of

B. JAIN PUBLISHERS (P) Ltd.

An ISO 9001 : 2000 Certified Company

1921/10, Chuna Mandi, Paharganj, New Delhi 110 055 (INDIA)

Tel.: +91-11-4567 1000 Fax: +91-11-4567 1010

Email: info@bjain.com Website: www.**pegasusforkids.com**

Printed in India

Characters in this story

Tara

A young bubbly girl with a fiery spirit

Krish

He is Tara's elder brother. He is a boy of 10 years who has a kind and caring nature.

Shweta

A shy, quiet girl who is Tara's best friend

Nikhil

A friend of Tara, Krish and Shweta

Roy

A friend of Tara, Krish and Shweta

Samir

A talented autistic boy who is in Tara's class

Mr. Rao

The secretary of the society

Mr. Soni

A grumpy and unfriendly elderly neighbour

Mrs. Soni

An extremely kind and good natured old lady

The Six Stars Club

"Krish....let's start a club," suggested Tara. "We should invite Roy, Nikhil and some more friends of ours," she continued without waiting for a reply.

"Sometimes school holidays can be so boring," said Krish. "Most of my friends have already gone on a vacation."

"Exactly!" said Tara. "That is why I suggested we do something. Shweta should be coming, any minute."

"Let's ask Mummy to phone Samir's mother," suggested Krish. "If she asks, I am sure Samir's mother will let him come..."

"Yes, and I will phone Roy and Nikhil," said Tara. "Great, we have a plan!"

Tara and Krish lived in an apartment building. There was a small compound, a sheltered car park and a garden in their building. The garden was small but really nice. It had two swings and a slide. It also had monkey bars and a small sand pit. The children liked to play there.

"We have a plan," started Krish when the children went down to the compound.

"Let me tell…let me tell…let me tell," shouted Tara jumping with her hands flapping like chicken wings. She was quite a sight to see.

Samir covered his ears. And the others looked on with a grin. Tara was the noisiest of the lot. When she was excited she had trouble keeping her voice down.

"Okay, so tell us," said Shweta, Tara's best friend. She

too lived in the same block of flats. They studied in the same class, same school.

"We have decided to start a club," said Tara.

"What a super idea," said Roy.

The children sat in the garden to discuss how to start up a club.

"First, we have to have a club house," said Krish. He noticed Tara's questioning look and continued, "We have to choose a place where we will meet. It must be a proper place where we can have our club meetings."

"Let's meet in the playground opposite the road," said Nikhil.

"Much sun...," said Samir softly. Samir was their school friend. He was an autistic child. He was poor at words, making language difficult for him. He did not speak like the rest of the children.

"So correct," said Roy.

"I think we should have a secret place...like the gardener's shed?" asked Shweta. "Maybe if we ask nicely he will let us use it."

"Yes, lets," said Krish.

The gardener was a nice, old man. He agreed to let them use the shed and even offered to help them clean the place. They all trooped to the shed. It was a small shed with a door and a window. You had to climb two steps to get in. From outside it looked very pretty because it had thick creeper plants growing on it. Inside there was a little cupboard in which the gardener kept his shears, hose and so on. The children promised not to touch the cupboard. Tara ran up to her house to get a broom and a duster. Between the gardener and the children, they had the shed clean in no time.

"Ah! The shed looks clean now," said Shweta. "My Mummy has an old rug. She said she doesn't need any more now that she has a new one. I will ask her to give it to us."

"Nice," said Samir softly.

"Okay. Let's call the meeting to order," said Krish. He knew a little about meetings as his Father was the member of the Rotary Club. The six children sat down and looked at Krish, waiting for him to continue. "We need to do a lot of things before we break for today," he continued. "We need a name for our club; we need to have a leader and a password."

"Let's call our club the Secret Six," suggested Roy.

"No," said Shweta. "That sounds too much like Enid

Blyton's Secret Seven!"

"Okay then…," said Nikhil, "let's call ourselves Silent Six."

"Nikhil!" said Tara with a surprised look on her face, "do you really think any club with me in it would be silent?"

"Sadly Six…Sane Six…Sagely Six ...Sacred Six."

"Silly," said Samir.

"Silly Six?" asked Tara.

"No," said Samir rocking away, "Silly names."

"Super Six?" asked Shweta.

"No. That sounds a little like Superman. What about Startling Six… or Sparkling Six," said Krish; he was the oldest of the lot and knew a lot of big words. "I know…," he said and then stopped midway. The rest of the children looked at him eagerly.

"Go on," said Tara impatiently.

"We are smart and we are bright. So let's call ourselves....The Six Stars," said Krish.

"Oh yes! That sounds super," said Shweta. "If all agree I can make star badges for the six of us. And we can wear them when we meet."

"That would be lovely," said Tara raising her hand in support. Immediately, the rest raised their hands too.

"Right then, that's decided. We are members of a club called The Six Stars," said Krish in a grand manner. "Now let's choose a leader."

"Yehhhhh, let's vote," said Tara.

"We will write the name of the person we want to be our leader on this piece of paper," said Krish. He then handed each of them a slip of paper. Tara and he had cut slips at home. They had also brought along a few pencils.

"I want to explain something to the members of The Six Stars. Firstly, no one can vote for themselves. Second, please think well before you write the name. A good leader is one who works well with everyone—both boys and girls. One who puts others before himself or herself," said Krish in a serious manner.

"Others before?" asked Samir not understanding. "Like in the bus line?"

"No," said Tara giggling. "It means that you must think of other peoples' need first, before your own needs. So a good leader should be fair, clever, caring and work well with others...okay? Now let's vote."

The six looked down at their paper. They thought hard

before they wrote the names. Then they folded the slips of paper and gave them to Krish. He opened the slips one by one and read out the names. "One vote for Roy, one vote and one more for Shweta, two for Krish, and one more for Shweta. That means Shweta got three votes, so she wins. I formally announce Shweta as the leader of our club."

Everybody clapped for her. Shweta blushed with happiness. She was so happy to be chosen as the leader of their newly formed club. "Thank you very much for voting for me. I promise to be a good leader," she said.

"Friends," she said in a formal manner. "We have to

decide on a password. But very quickly as it is nearly lunchtime."

"What about, twinkling stars…or twinkle twinkle… shining… like stars," suggested Krish.

"Shall we make the password 'twinkle twinkle'?" asked Tara.

All agreed by putting their hands up. Only Samir was a bit confused. "Pass...word?" he asked. "What for… passwo..rd?"

"Samir, when we want to enter the club house we have to say our password. Only when you say 'twinkle twinkle' will you be let in. This way we will know whether the person at the door is a member or not," explained Krish very patiently.

"Right, then that's decided," said Shweta. "The name of our club is The Six Stars. Our password is 'twinkle twinkle'. We will end the meeting today. And meet at ten-thirty tomorrow morning. Please be on time."

They all got up and said their good-byes. Krish carefully shut the door as he was the last to leave.

"What are you doing in there?" a loud voice boomed. It was their ground floor neighbour, Mr. Soni. "Go away; I don't like little children wandering about."

The six were very frightened. Samir held Krish's hand as they all ran off.

The club house looked nicer the next day. Shweta, who had come early, had laid out the rug. She had even got an old pencil holder to put the pencils. Krish and Tara had cleaned the window, the evening before. Now the sun shone through the clean glass and the shed looked much brighter.

Each of them said the password 'twinkle twinkle' and came in. It was fun to be a part of a club. The children were very eager to start the meeting. Samir, however, was the happiest of the lot. This was the first time he was asked to be in a group. He had practiced the password all evening.

"Mummy went batty. Last evening," said Samir slowly.

"Why?" asked Krish urging him on. He knew that Samir had to try hard to talk to people.

"I was practicing. Twink..le twink..le," said Samir. "And Rhea, my little sister...sang twink..le twin...k...le little star. Every time!" He had a cheeky smile on his face.

The six started laughing loudly. And Samir started clapping his hands.

"Good. We must decide what we want to do, now that we have started a club. We do have fun playing but I

think we should do some good work too. That way everybody will be proud of us," said Shweta.

"Ohh! What a good leader you make," said Tara.

"Anybody has any ideas?" said Shweta, blushing.

"Let's make birdfeeders. My Mummy was saying the sparrows are disappearing from Mumbai," said Roy.

"Let's do something that stops big children from bullying little ones," said Nikhil.

"We can start a clean-up our city campaign," said Krish.

"Make others happy," said Tara.

"Stop smoking," said Samir. Smoke really irritated him.

"What?" asked Roy shocked. "You smoke?"

"No, he means get other people to stop smoking," said Tara. She sat next to him in class. So slowly she had began to understand his muddled talk. She knew what he was trying to say.

"Oh!" said Roy, much relieved.

"All good ideas," said Shweta. "I think we can do most of them. Let's start with making a birdhouse tomorrow. Anybody has an idea how to make one?"

"We will need empty plastic bottles. Some strings to tie it on the tree. Scissors, sticks …and waterproof pens," said Krish.

"And seeds and sticks. Like ice cream sticks," added Tara. She had helped her brother make a birdfeeder for his class project.

"Okay. So let's get all this stuff tomorrow and make

bird feeders," said Shweta. "That reminds me," she continued, looking into her bag. "I made these badges for us." She took out the badges and handed them to the rest.

"Wowieeeee!" exclaimed Tara loudly. "Super duper."

The badges were very smart. Shweta had taken some stars left over from last year's Christmas decorations. She had then, with her Mother's help, stitched on safety pins in the back. The children pinned the star on their t-shirts. Now they all looked as if they belonged to a group.

"Now the next plan," said Shweta. "I liked Tara's idea of making others happy. But how can we do that?

"Yes, let's do things for others," said Nikhil.

"Like?" asked Shweta.

They could not think of anything, they sat thinking quietly.

"Oh! Forgot," said Samir taking out some sweets.

"Mummy gave. For you."

"Samir already did something for others. He got us sweets. That is so nice of you. Thank you very much," said Shweta.

"I know let's be nice to everyone. Let's give everyone we meet a smile," suggested Tara. "That way we can spread happiness."

"That's a good idea," said Krish.

"Next?" asked Shweta.

"Stop smoking… stop smoking," said Samir.

"What can we do to stop people from smoking?" asked Krish. "Think…think."

"It is not possible to go and tell adults," said Roy.

"Let's make posters," said Tara.

"That's a good idea. We can ask Samir to draw for us and then we can do the writing," suggested Krish.

"I will go up and get the paper and paints from home," said Tara.

"I think, I'd better help her," said Nikhil, getting up. Both the children ran off to get the stuff they needed to make the posters. They were back soon.

"Guess, who we met on our way down?" asked Tara. "Mr. Grouchy," she said without waiting for the rest to reply.

"Mr. Grouchy?" asked Roy, totally mystified.

"Mr. Grouchy is our ground floor neighbour. His real name is Mr. Soni. Remember the old gentleman who yelled at us when we were going home yesterday? That person! Shweta and I call him Mr. Grouchy," she said, all in one breath.

"Oh!" said Shweta a bit nervously. She did not like Mr. Soni very much because he was mean to kids. He was forever yelling at them not to make noise. He did not like kids standing at the gate and talking. He did not like festivals because he thought they were noisy. He did not like holidays because then kids would be playing in the garden all day long. Oh! The list was endless.

"Well, as usual he bellowed and said, 'I don't like kids running around. And why are you making so much noise? Whatever are you doing in the shed? I am sure you are up to some mischief. I shall complain.' Poor Nikhil. He was so scared he just stood there and I...," said Tara.

"You did what?" asked Krish.

"I said, 'Good morning Mr. Soni' and smiled at him. He didn't smile back, but instead hollered 'Missy, don't be cheeky.' Can you believe that, Krish?" said Tara. "I wasn't being cheeky. Was I? I just wanted to be nice to him. Remember we said we would try to make others happy? Smiling is a way to pass happiness, isn't it?"

"Yes," said Samir. He was trying hard to understand what Tara was saying. "We should smile."

"We stood there for a moment and then walked away. But you know Samir is so correct. Smoke is not nice. Mr. Soni was smoking and the passage smelled ever so much," said Nikhil.

"Here is all the stuff. And Mummy gave me some cookies to share with you," said Tara. "Krish, mummy asked me to send you up to get the lemonade she has made for us."

After they had the cookies and the lemonade they sat and brainstormed ideas for their posters.

Soon they had two posters ready....

One poster had the drawing of the earth with children around it. The children were not just standing, they were cleaning up. For example, one had a broom in his hand, a girl was picking up a crumpled paper; a pair of children were watering a plant and so on. It read 'Save our Earth; Keep it Clean'. The second poster was very interesting. Samir had drawn a huge hand holding the earth. A small plant was growing from the earth. Around the drawing the children wrote 'Keep the Air Clean', 'Stop Smoking', 'Don't Waste Water', 'Pick up your Litter' and 'Don't Cut Trees'.

"Wow! They look good," said Shweta. She noticed Roy sitting a little away drawing on a sheet of paper. "Roy, you have drawn a poster on your own! That's great."

The rest turned to look at it. It was a fine poster. It had a drawing of a little girl standing holding a doll. She had tears flowing down her face like rain. In the

picture there was a sad faced sun, gloomy clouds and a road sign which had 'Bullying' written on it. Only, the sign had a huge red cross on the word 'bully'. The poster read, 'Do Not Ever, Ever Hurt a Child'.

"This is a fantastic poster," said Krish. "We are goooood, aren't we? I do think we are shining stars."

"Now we will have to find the correct place to put up these posters. But I think, we should ask the building secretary before putting them up," said Shweta. "We don't want to be a nuisance, do we?"

"That's a good idea," agreed Roy. "Can I take one poster for my building?" he asked.

After asking for permission, the children put up the posters on the building notice board. The next day they made the birdfeeders. And those were hung too. They suspended them on the trees that grew in the compound. Roy, Samir and Nikhil took one each for their apartments, too. The children were very happy to spend their time well. It was a good club, they had started.

One morning, a week later, a notice was sent to each of the flats in Krish's and Tara's building. It read 'All the flat owner's are requested to attend a meeting at 6:00 pm. The meeting will take place in the parking lot.' At 6:00 pm sharp everyone was there, including the childrens' fathers.

Without any nicety or any greetings, Mr. Soni started shouting. "This has to stop. There are children all over the building all day long. They make much noise and laugh all the time. They laugh at me. Now they have even put up birdfeeders. So the birds are making so much noise. They have put up posters telling me not to smoke. This is too much."

Everybody was taken aback.

"Calm down, Mr. Soni," said Mr. Rao, the building

secretary. “Let’s listen to everybody and get down to the real problem.”

“Call the gardener, let’s hear what he has to say,” yelled Mr. Soni.

So the gardener was called. He gave the children a clean chit. He said that the children had cleaned the shed and that the children also helped him clean the garden. He added that they did not create trouble for him. In fact, they were a great help.

“What about the nasty posters?” asked Mr. Soni.

Most of the adults did not have a problem with the

posters. Especially since the children had first taken permission from Mr. Rao before putting it up.

"As for the birdfeeders," said Mrs. Rao, "I think it is such a kind gesture to feed the hungry birds."

"Mr. Soni, I do not think any of this was especially done to offend you," said Mr. Rao. "I think the children are very well behaved and do not get in the way of any of us. I think, they have the right to play in the garden and compound. I think their club, as they call it, is harmless. They have the right to sit and play together if it is not hurting or harming anybody."

"Besides, I think they are very sweet

and polite children," said Mrs. Soni quietly. "They always smile and wish you when they see you. The other day they even carried my grocery to my flat and they did not even wait for me to thank them properly."

To make the long story short, the adults agreed that the club could stay. It was also decided that the children could use the shed. The children of The Six Stars club have a lot of fun. Maybe you could start a club like them? Do you think you would like that?

The Convention on the Rights of the Child

The United Nations Convention on the Rights of the Child (UNCRC) is an international human rights agreement that provides all children and young people (below the age of 18) a wide-ranging set of rights. 'Rights' are things every child should have or be able to do freely. All children have the same rights. These rights are fixed by The Convention on the Rights of the Child. Almost all countries have agreed to follow them.

All children and young people have the same rights regardless of their religion, language, skin colour, whether they are a boy or a girl or where they are from. These rights cover what children need to survive, stay safe and be protected from all forms of physical and mental violence, including cruel, inhuman treatment or punishment. Every child has the right to an education which develops their personality, talents and abilities to the full. These rights support children to have opportunities to lead stable, rewarding lives.
They are all connected with each other and all are important.

Article 1

Everyone under 18 has these rights.

Article 2

All children have these rights, no matter who they are, where they live, what their parents do, what language they speak, what their religion is, whether they are a boy or girl, what their culture is, whether they have a disability, whether they are rich or poor. No child should be treated unfairly on any basis.

Article 3

All adults should do what is best for you. When adults make decisions, they should think about how their decisions will affect children.

Article 5

Your family has the responsibility to help you learn to exercise your rights, and to ensure that your rights are protected.

Article 12

You have the right to give your opinion, and for adults to listen and take it seriously.

Article 13

You have the right to find out things and share and express what you think with others. You can do this by talking, drawing, writing or in any other way. You must remember that your actions should not harm or offend anyone else.

Article 15

You have the right to join clubs or organisations, or even set up your own. You can do this as long as it does not stop other people from enjoying their rights. You also have the right to meet with other people. This is the right of the child to freedom of association and to freedom of peaceful assembly.

Article 42

You have the right to know your rights! Adults should know about these rights and help you learn about them, too.

There is a close connection between rights and responsibilities. All people, including children, have responsibilities to uphold and promote children's rights

You have the right to expression that is you have a right to say what you think and for adults and children take it seriously. If you have the rights to express yourself you have the responsibility to listen. You must listen carefully and respectfully to all children and adults as you also want everyone to listen and respect what I have to say.

You also have the responsibility to stand up for your rights and the rights of other children. Likewise you have a responsibility to follow the rules at home, at school and in the community; after all they are there for your safety and to protect your rights and the rights of others.

Titles in this series

About the author:

Swaroop Rawal, the author of this series is a multi-faceted personality. She began her career in the world of glamour by winning the Ms India title and soon landed in the glittering world of television and films. After a very successful career there, she slowly pulled herself out of the acting world and got married to veteran actor Paresh Rawal. Together, they have raised two sons.

Within a span of a few years, Swaroop took a remarkable step to develop another career. She worked on her PhD which focused on education, drama and learning disabilities. Rawal received her doctoral degree in 2006 from the University of Worcester in the United Kingdom. Her thesis was titled: The role of drama in enhancing life skills in children with specific learning difficulties in a Mumbai school: My reflective account.

She recently wrote a book titled **Learning Disabilities in a Nutshell: Dyslexia, Dysgraphia, Dyscalculia, Dyspraxia** published by B. Jain Publishers, New Delhi. She describes the book as an introduction to various forms of learning disabilities to parents. The foreword of this much talked about book is written by renowned actor Aamir Khan after his directorial debut in the film 'Taare Zameen Pe'.

For the past two years, Rawal travels to Gandhinagar in Gujarat where she provides training to teachers using drama techniques on issues including creative thinking, decision making, problem solving, understanding emotions and also coping with stress. Her current training programme in Gujarat focuses on all children, and not just those suffering from learning disabilities.